This collection published in Great Britain 2003 by Walker Books Ltd
87 Vauxhall Walk, London SE11 5HJ

2 4 6 8 10 9 7 5 3 1

This book has been typeset in Charlotte and Utopia

Printed in Italy

British Library Cataloguing in Publication Data:
a catalogue record for this book is available from the British Library

ISBN 0-7445-9629-7

Baby and Toddler Treasury

Stories and Fun for the Very Young

WALKER BOOKS

AND SUBSIDIARIES

LONDON • BOSTON • SYDNEY

Contents

A You're Adorable

A you're a-dor-a-ble, B you're so beau-ti-ful, C you're a cu-tie full of charms,

D you're a dar-ling and E you're ex-cit-ing and F you're a feath-er in my arms.

G you look good to me, H you're so hea-ven-ly, I you're the one I i-dol-ize,

J we're like Jack and Jill, K you're so kiss-a-ble, L is the love-light in your eyes.

A song by Buddy Kaye, Fred Wise and Sidney Lippman

M, N, O, P, I could go on — all day. Q, R,

S, T, al-pha-bet-i-cally speak-ing you're O-K! — U made my life com-plete,

V means you're ver-y sweet, W——— X, Y, Z— It's

fun to wan-der through the al-pha-bet with you to tell you what you mean to me!—

illustrated by Martha Alexander

What does a baby do?

jumble

juggle

jump

bang

burp

bump

totter

tumble

throw

gurgle

giggle

grow

by Catherine and Laurence Anholt

What are babies like?

Babies kick
and babies crawl,

Slide their potties down the hall.

Babies smile
and babies yell,

This one has
a funny smell.

Grey plane

CHARLOTTE VOAKE'S

COLOURS

PURPLE

RED

Brown
trailer

Red
tru

Green tractor

12

Blue train

ORANGE

Black

BLUE

YELLOW

PINK

BROWN

GREEN

Yellow boat

Pink car

Black bike

Getting Dressed

T-shirt

shorts

scarf

gloves

sandals

sun-hat

boots

coat

dress

Who is dressed for a hot day?

by Catherine and Laurence Anholt

vest

jumper

cardigan

pants

trousers

socks

shoes

Who is dressed for a cold day?

I LOVE Animals

by Flora McDonnell

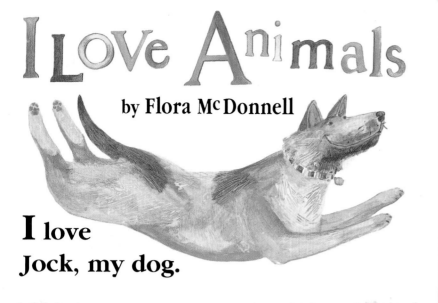

I love
Jock, my dog.

I love the ducks
waddling to the water.

I love
the donkey
braying
"hee-haw!"

I love
the pony
rolling
over and
over.

I love the turkey
strutting round
the yard.

I love the pig with all her little piglets.

I love the hens hopping up and down.

I love the cow swishing her tail.

I love the goat racing across the field.

love the sheep bleating o her lamb.

I love all the animals.

I hope they love me.

MOTHER GOOSE

LITTLE BOY BLUE

Little Boy Blue,
   Come blow your horn,
The sheep's in the meadow,
   The cow's in the corn;
But where is the boy
   Who looks after the sheep?
He's under a haycock,
   Fast asleep.
Will you wake him?
   No, not I,
For if I do,
   He's sure to cry.

Three poems illustrated by
Michael Foreman

TO THE MAGPIE

Magpie, magpie, flutter and flee,
Turn up your tail and good luck come to me.

BAA, BAA, BLACK SHEEP

Baa, baa, black sheep,
    Have you any wool?
Yes sir, yes sir,
    Three bags full:
One for the master,
    And one for the dame,
And one for the little boy
    Who lives down the lane.

19

My Cat Jack

by Patricia Casey

My cat Jack is a yawning cat.
He's a stretching-down cat. He's a stretching-up cat.

My cat Jack is a scratching cat.
He's a curling cat. He's a lapping cat.

My cat Jack is a purring cat,
a rough-tongued cat, a washing cat.

He's a cat who likes washing all over.

My cat Jack is a playing cat.
He's a pouncing cat. He's an acrobat cat.

And sometimes he's a silly old cat.
I love him, my cat Jack.

Mum's Home

Mum's home.

And what else?

Have a banana ...

by Jan Ormerod

Things for a baby.

What's in her basket?

Dig deep.   Blow Mum's nose.

and a snooze.

HUMPTY DUMPTY

illustrated by Julie Lacome

Humpty Dumpty
Sat on a wall,
Humpty Dumpty
Had a great fall.

All the king's horses
And all the king's men
Couldn't put Humpty
Together again.

abc

illustrated by Ian Beck

Aa

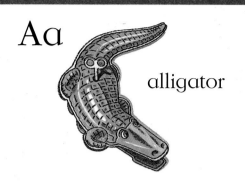

alligator

Bb

bear

Cc

camel

Gg

giraffe

Hh

hippopotamus

Ii

iguana

Nn

newt

Oo

ostrich

Pp

penguin

Tt

tiger

Uu

unicorn

Vv

vulture

Ww

walrus

26

Dd

dolphin

Ee

elephant

Ff

flamingos

Jj

jaguar

Kk

kangaroo

Ll

lion

Mm

monkey

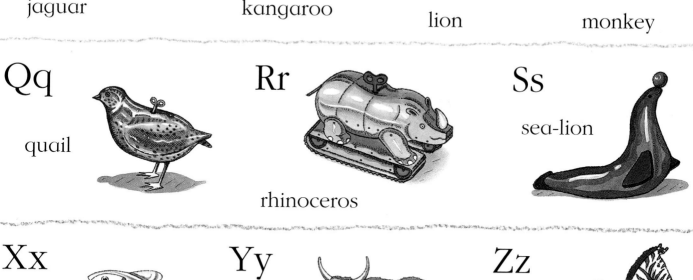

Qq

quail

Rr

rhinoceros

Ss

sea-lion

Xx

x-ray fish

Yy

yak

Zz

zebra

One, two,
Buckle my shoe;

Three, four,
Knock at the door;

Five, six,
Pick up sticks;

Seven, eight,
Lay them straight;

Nine, ten,
A big fat hen;

MY SHOE

illustrated by
Charlotte Voake

Eleven, twelve,
Dig and delve;

Thirteen, fourteen,
Maids a-courting;

Fifteen, sixteen,
Maids in the kitchen;

Seventeen, eighteen,
Maids in waiting;

Nineteen, twenty,
My plate's empty.

FISHERMAN

Heave ho!
Away we go.

Rub-a-dub,
scour and scrub.

Net's full,
tug and pull.

Lower the catch,
down the hatch.

by Paul Manning   *illustrated by* Nicola Bayley

Mind that plate –
too late!

Achooo!
Wet through.

Prepare the buoy.
Land ahoy!

Heave a sigh,
home and dry.

31

When We Went to the Park

by Shirley Hughes

When Grandpa and I put on our coats and went to the park…

1 We saw one black cat sitting on a wall,

2  Two big girls licking ice-creams,

3

Three ladies chatting on a bench,

4

Four babies in buggies,

5  Five children playing in the sandpit,

6

Six runners running,

7

Seven dogs chasing one another,

8

Eight boys kicking a ball,

9

Nine ducks swimming on the pond,

10

Ten birds swooping in the sky, and so many leaves
that I couldn't count them all.

On the way back we saw
the black cat again.
Then we went home for tea.

Things
I Like

by Anthony Browne

This is me and this is what I like:

Painting …
and riding my bike.

Playing with toys,
and dressing up.

Making a cake …
and watching TV.

Going to birthday
parties, and being
with my friends.

Having a bath …
hearing a
bedtime story …

Climbing trees …
and kicking a ball.

Hiding …
and acrobatics.

and dreaming.

Bumpety Bump

A Knee-ride Rhyme

by Kathy Henderson   *illustrated by Carol Thompson*

The baby went for a ride,
***a-bumpety-
bumpety-bump!***

She rode in her sister's arms,
***a-slumpety-
slumpety-slump!***

She rode on her
grandpa's knee,
***a-tumpety-
tumpety-tump!***

She rode on her mother's hip,
**_a-lumpety-
lumpety-lump!_**

She rode on her uncle's neck,
**_a-humpety-
humpety-hump!_**

And flew high up in the air,
**_a-jumpety-
jumpety-jump!_**

She rode around and
about and then …
went back to sleep
in her cot again.

Clara Vulliamy   Blue Hat

orange gloves

blue hat

red coat

brown jumper

Red Coat

black shoes

green socks

purple trousers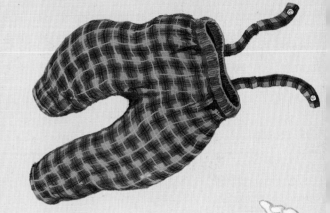

 pink T-shirt

yellow vest

 white nappy

… all gone!

Where's My Mummy?

Jill the Farmer
and her friends

by Nick Butterworth

Pete is a mechanic.

What does he use?

Betty is a baker.

What does she sell?

Fred is a dustman.

What does he collect?

Anna is a doctor.

Why has she come?

Jim is a messenger.

What does he ride?

Four black puppies in a basket, fast asleep.

One black puppy
waking up.

One black puppy
going for a walk.

PUPPIES

by **Sally Grindley** illustrated by **Clive Scruton**

One black puppy
pulling at an apron.

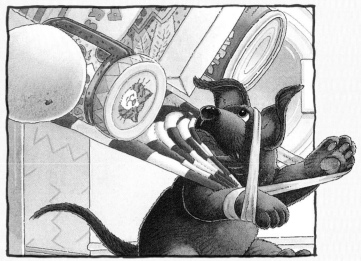

One shopping basket
falling down.

CRASH!

45

Three black puppies running in to have a look.

Three black puppies
see … A GHOST!

One white puppy chasing
three black puppies.

All four puppies running
round and round.

All four puppies
running back to bed.

All four puppies in a basket, fast asleep.

Hey Diddle, Diddle

illustrated by Rosemary Wells

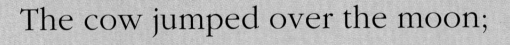

Hey diddle, diddle,

the cat and the fiddle,

The cow jumped over the moon;

The little dog laughed

to see such fun,

And the dish ran away

with the spoon.

cluck baa

hiss

cluck

hoot

croak

neigh

50

by John Burningham

quack

moo

roar

buzz

baa

Let's

Can you find your ears?

Can you bite your toes?

Can you find your eyes?

by Amy MacDonald

52

Do It

Can you play peek-a-boo?

Can you touch your nose?

Can you wave bye-bye?

illustrated by Maureen Roffey

OLD MOTHER HUBBARD

**Old Mother Hubbard
Went to the cupboard,**

To fetch her poor dog a bone;
But when she got there
The cupboard was bare
And so the poor dog had none.

She went to the baker's
To buy him some bread;
But when she came back
The poor dog was dead.

She went to the fishmonger
To buy him some fish;
But when she came back
He was licking the dish.

She went to the undertaker's
To buy him a coffin;
But when she came back
The poor dog was laughing.

She took a clean dish
To get him some tripe;
But when she came back
He was smoking a pipe.

She went to the hatter's
To buy him a hat;
But when she came back
He was feeding the cat.

illustrated by Elizabeth Wood

She went to the tailor's
To buy him a coat;
But when she came back
He was riding a goat.

She went to the cobbler's
To buy him some shoes;
But when she came back
He was reading the news.

She went to the seamstress
To buy him some linen;
But when she came back
The dog was a-spinning.

She went to the barber's
To buy him a wig;
But when she came back
He was dancing a jig.

She went to the hosier's
To buy him some hose;
But when she came back
He was dressed in his clothes.

The dame made a curtsey,
The dog made a bow;
The dame said, *"Your servant,"*
The dog said, *"Bow-wow."*

Toddlerobics

by Zita Newcome

Hats off, coats off, all rush in,
everybody ready for toddler gym!

Heads and shoulders, knees and toes.
Eyes and ears, mouth and nose.

Flap your arms up and down.
Lift your feet off the ground.

Stretch up high and touch the sky,
bend down low and touch your toes.

Lift that rattle in the air,
shake it, shake it, everywhere!

Clap your hands, stamp your feet.
Nod your head, dance to the beat.

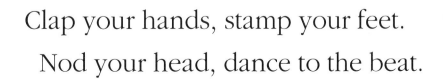

All join together to make a puffer train,
stretch out your arms and zoom like a plane.

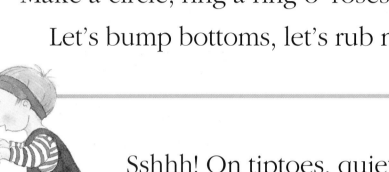

Make a circle, ring a ring o' roses.
Let's bump bottoms, let's rub noses.

Sshhh! On tiptoes, quiet as a mouse.
Now great big steps all round the house.

Turning, twirling, like a spinning top.
Bump on your bottom when it's time to stop.

Wriggle your toes, crawl like a cat,
now lie down and stretch out flat.

Toddlerobics is lots of fun.
See you next week, everyone!

Noah's Ark

A long time ago there lived a man called Noah.

Noah was a good man, who trusted in God.

There were also many wicked people in the world.

God wanted to punish the wicked people,

so he said to Noah…

I shall make a flood of water and wash all
the wicked people away. Build an ark for
your family and all the animals.

Noah worked for years and years
and years to build the ark.

At last the ark was finished.

Noah and his
family gathered
lots of food.

Then the animals came,

two by two,

two by two,

into the ark.

retold and illustrated by Lucy Cousins

When the ark was full Noah felt a drop of rain. It rained and rained and rained. It rained for forty days and forty nights. The world was covered with water. At last the rain stopped and the sun came out. Noah sent a dove to find dry land. The dove came back with a leafy twig. "Hurrah!" shouted Noah. "The flood has ended." But many more days passed before the ark came to rest on dry land. Then Noah and all the animals came safely out of the ark, and life began again on the earth.

61

NUMBERS

ONE, Two, three, four, five,
Once I caught a fish alive,
Six, seven, eight, nine, ten,
Then I let it go again.

illustrated by Charlotte Voake

Why did you let it go?
Because it bit my finger so.
Which finger did it bite?
This little finger on the right.

Bumps-a-daisy

Eyes,

nose,

hands,

knees,

by Colin and Jacqui Hawkins

and *bumps-a-daisy!*

Pets

by Louise Voce

dog

goldfish

hamster

gerbil

rabbit

mouse

guinea-pig

budgie

tortoise

cat

Sleeping

peeping

tickling

climbing up

by Jan Ormerod

bouncing

pulling his nose

cuddling

I LIKE BOOKS

I like books.
Funny books
and scary books.
Fairy tales and
nursery rhymes.
Comic books and
colouring books.
Fat books
and thin books.

by Anthony Browne

Books about
dinosaurs,
and books about
monsters.
Counting books
and alphabet
books.

Books about space,
and books
about pirates.
Song books
and strange books.

Yes, I really
do like books.

The Wheels on the Bus

The wheels on the bus go round and round,
Round and round, round and round,
The wheels on the bus go round and round,
All day long.

The grans on the bus
go knit, knit,
knit…

The children on the bus
go wriggle, wriggle,
wriggle…

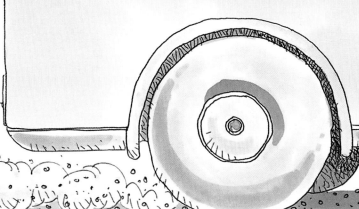

illustrated by Toni Goffe

The dads
on the bus
go nod, nod,
nod…

The mums
on the bus
go chatter, chatter,
chatter…

The wipers
on the bus
go swish, swish
swish…

The horn on the bus
goes beep, beep,
beep…

The driver on the bus
goes bother, bother,
bother…

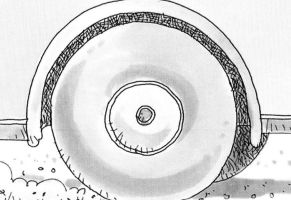

73

Lizzie and her kitty

by David Martin *illustrated by Debi Gliori*

Where is Lizzie?
Lizzie's in her chair.

Where is Lizzie's pudding?
Dripping from her hair.

Where is Lizzie's kitty?
Kitty's on the floor.

Kitty's licking pudding
And hoping for some more.

Now where is Lizzie?

Lizzie's at the sink.

She's turning on the water
So she can get a drink.

Now where is kitty?
With Lizzie in her chair.

And what is kitty doing?
Licking Lizzie's hair.

Let's make a noise

Let's make a noise like a dog.

WOOF

Let's make a noise like a train.

TOOT, TOOT

Let's make a noise like a cat.

MEOW

76

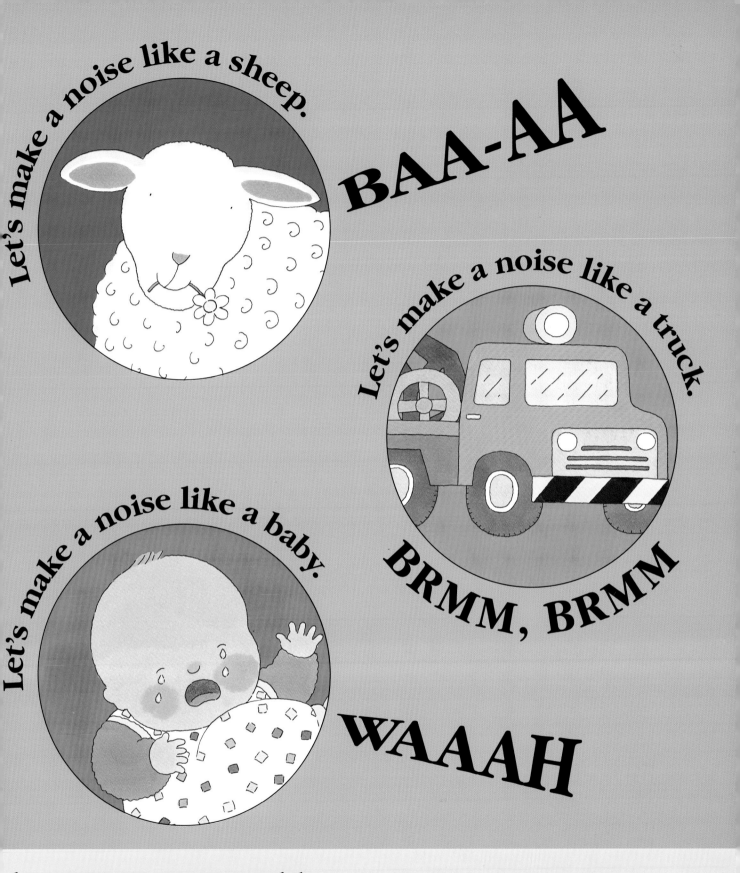

Let's make a noise like a sheep.

BAA-AA

Let's make a noise like a truck.

BRMM, BRMM

Let's make a noise like a baby.

WAAAH

by Amy MacDonald
illustrated by Maureen Roffey

77

Baby Animals on the Farm

horse
and foal

sheep and
lambs

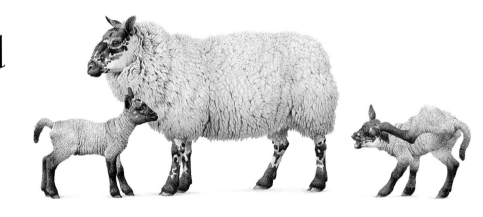

duck and
ducklings

  cow
and calf

pig and
piglets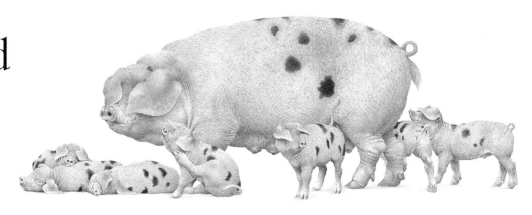

  chickens
and
chicks

79

Being Together

Telling a secret,
Listening with care,

Bending down low,
Stretching high in the air.

Dancing to music,
Feeling the beat,

Lying flat on our backs
And kicking our feet.

by Shirley Hughes

Laughing,
(Always a good thing to do),

Reading out loud,
Reading to you.

Sharing a sandwich,
A new place to hide.

Love and kisses
And two smiles wide!

Pat·A·Cake

Pat-a-cake, pat-a-cake,
baker's man,
Bake me a cake
as fast as you can.
Pat it, and prick it,
and mark it with b,
And put it in the oven
for baby and me!

illustrated by Tony Kenyon

Goodnight

Messy dinner cleared away,
Toys packed up for another day,
Now it's bathtime, taking off clothes,
Wriggly, giggly, tickly toes.

Splashy water, boats in a storm,
Out you get, cuddle up warm,
Nice clean teeth, clever baby!
Nice clean nappy, pyjamas, maybe?

Bedtime story, sleepyhead,
It's getting late, time for bed,
Goodnight, moon, shining bright,
Goodnight, room, cosy light.

Snuggle down, no need to cry,
One more song, a lullaby,
Goodnight, bear, can't help yawning,
Goodnight, baby, see you in the morning.

by Clara Vulliamy

Billy's Boot

Let's put the toys away, Billy.

Billy help Lily.

Spot and Slinky go in the basket, ball in basket too.

by Martha Alexander

It's all done, Billy.

All done!

Where's your boot, Billy?

Boot, Lily!

Hush, Little Baby

Hush, little baby, don't say a word,
Papa's going to buy you a mocking bird.

If the mocking bird won't sing,
Papa's going to buy you a diamond ring.

If the diamond ring turns to brass,
Papa's going to buy you a looking-glass.

If the looking-glass gets broke,
Papa's going to buy you a billy-goat.

If that billy-goat runs away,
Papa's going to buy you another today.

illustrated by Julie Lacome

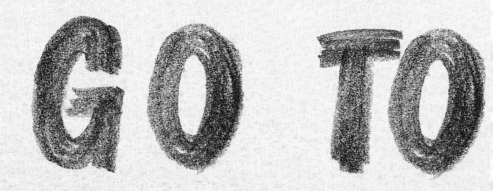

It was time for Bartholomew to go to bed.

"Ba, time for bed,"
George said.

"Nah!" said
Bartholomew.

Nah

George said, "Brush your
teeth and go to bed."
"Nah!" said Bartholomew.

BED!

by
**Virginia
Miller**

"Have you brushed
your teeth yet, Ba?"
"Nah!" said Bartholomew,
beginning to cry.

"Come on, Ba, into bed!"
George said.
"Nah!" said Bartholomew.
"Nah, nah, nah, nah,
NAH!" said Bartholomew.

"Go to bed!"

George said in a big voice.
Bartholomew got into bed.

He giggled and wriggled, he hid and tiggled,

he cuddled and huggled, he snuggled and sighed.

"Goodnight, Bartholomew," said George.
"Nah," said Bartholomew softly.
He gave a big yawn, closed his eyes
and went to sleep.